BLACKBERRY FARM

THE BIRTHDAY PICNIC

Jane Pilgrim

This edition first published in the United Kingdom in 2000 by
Brockhampton Press
20 Bloomsbury Street
London WC1B 3QA
a member of the Caxton Publishing Group

Designed and Produced for Brockhampton Press by
Open Door Limited
80 High Street, Colsterworth, Lincolnshire, NG33 5JA

Illustrator: F. Stocks May
Colour separation: GA Graphics Stamford

Title: BLACKBERRY FARM, The Birthday Picnic
ISBN: 1-84186-049-2

THE BIRTHDAY PICNIC

Jane Pilgrim

Illustrated by F. Stocks May

BROCKHAMPTON PRESS

It was Mrs Nibble's birthday and everyone at Blackberry Farm was very excited because Mrs Smiles, the farmer's wife was giving a special Birthday Picnic for her. Everyone was invited, and Joe Robin delivered all the invitations himself.

Rosy's present was a beautiful big carrot, Posy's a large, luscious lettuce, and Christopher's a warm woolly scarf which Lucy Mouse had knitted. Mrs Nibble was very pleased.

After breakfast she dressed the
little bunnies in their best clothes,
and they all went up to the
farmyard to join everyone else –
because it was to be a dinner
picnic, with games first.

In the farmyard Mrs Smiles was waiting with Joy and Bob (her two children). "I'm very sorry, Mrs Nibble," she said, "but Mr Smiles and Mr Nibble are so busy today that they may be late for your party. But all the others are here and the food is packed, so I think we will start."

And she led the way out of the
farmyard, followed by Joy and Bob
and all the animals.

At the end of the lane from
Blackberry Farm there is a big
field, and this is where the
Birthday Picnic was to be.
Mrs Smiles and Joy and Bob
put the baskets of food down
under a big, shady tree, and Rusty
the Sheepdog spread the
table-cloth out.

"Now we will play some games," said Mrs Smiles. "We will start with Oranges and Lemons. Henry, will you and Emily be the archway?" So Henry the Pig and Emily the Goat made the archway, and they all played Oranges and Lemons.

"Now we will play 'Here we come gathering nuts in May'," said Mrs Smiles – and she divided the animals up into two lines.

It was very exciting when Lucy
Mouse was sent to fetch Little
Mary Hen away, because they
pulled and pulled and pulled,
and neither could pull quite
hard enough. So Bob said he
thought they had all better stop
and have dinner.

They all sat down and watched
Mrs Smiles and Joy unpack the
baskets. What a lovely dinner it
was – sandwiches, pies, sausages,
apples, jellies and bananas, and of
course lots of lemonade to drink.

George the Kitten was so excited
that he seized two sausages and
ran up the tree before Ernest Owl
could scold him for his bad
manners. Then Mrs Squirrel and
Hazel thought they would be more
comfortable up the tree, too, and
so they followed him, and
everyone ate a very big dinner.

After dinner Mrs Nibble insisted
on Rosy, Posy and Christopher
having a rest. "That is a very
sensible idea," quacked Walter
Duck, and he tucked his head in
under his wing – and everyone
slept until tea-time.

And then came the big birthday surprise for Mrs Nibble. Mr Smiles and Mr Nibble arrived with a big box, which they carefully put down in front of her. "Happy birthday, Mrs Nibble," they said, "and many, many happy returns from all of us at Blackberry Farm. Here is your present."

Mrs Nibble bent to open it.
Inside was a beautiful muslin
apron and a beautiful muslin cap
with ribbons.